RAW

USBORNE

QUEST of the GODS

With thanks to Adrian Bott

First published in the UK in 2012 by Usborne Publishing Ltd.,
Usborne House, 83-85 Saffron Hill, London EC1N 8RT, England.
www.usborne.com

Cover illustration by Jerry Parris. Inside illustrations by David Shephard.
Map by Ian McNee.

The name Usborne and the devices ♀ ⊕ are Trade Marks of
Usborne Publishing Ltd.

A CIP catalogue record for this book is available from the British Library.

ISBN 9781409557111   JFMAM JASOND/12 02359/1
Printed in Dongguan, Guangdong, China.

THE PROPHECY OF THE SPHINX

THE SPHINX AM I
GUARDIAN OF THE PYRAMIDS
KEEPER OF SECRETS

THE PAST I REMEMBER
THE PRESENT I SEE
THE FUTURE I FORETELL

WHEN THE PHARAOH SHALL DIE
AT THE HANDS OF HIS SON
A PLAGUE SHALL FALL UPON EGYPT

THE LORD OF STORMS WILL RISE AGAIN
THE GOOD GODS WILL BE CHAINED
AND MONSTERS WILL WALK THE LAND

THE SACRED RIVER SHALL SLOW AND DRY
THE SUN WILL SCORCH THE LAND LIKE FIRE
THE STREETS OF EGYPT SHALL RUN WITH BLOOD

BUT HOPE WILL COME FROM THE SOUTH
A HERO OF THE WHEATFIELDS
A KING WITHOUT A KINGDOM

THE LAST OF HIS FAMILY
A LOST CHILD OF HORUS
HE SHALL BATTLE THE MONSTERS TO FREE THE GODS

HE WILL CLAIM THE WHITE CROWN
HE WILL CLAIM THE RED CROWN
HE WILL RULE ALL EGYPT

THE SPHINX AM I
THESE SECRETS I SHARE
GUARD THEM WELL

MANU'S MAP OF ANCIENT EGYPT

NILE DELTA

Heliopolis

Giza

Saqqara

RED SEA

Temple of Set

EASTERN DESERT

Nubt

HIGH DESERT

Waset and Karnak

Entrance to the
Underworld

Temple of Horus

Nebyt

Fortress of Fire

THE NILE

N

S

SAHARA DESERT

PROLOGUE

It was early morning and the sun was rising. The guards patrolling the palace walls were already sweating in the Egyptian heat. But no natural light ever reached the private bedchamber of Oba the Pharaoh. The windows were shuttered and barred. The room was steeped in darkness. The only light came from a metal fire basket in its very centre, heaped with burning charcoal. It filled the room with a ghoulish glow, making the ornate fittings gleam red and causing hungry shadows to lick at the walls. The room was piled with riches and ornaments, all stolen from Oba's own people.

The boy Pharaoh was as vain as he was wicked. Like all young Egyptian men, he scented his body with perfume. Hundreds of bottles and ointment pots glimmered on his dressing table. The room was suffocatingly hot, and the smell of myrrh was overpowering.

Oba lounged on a pyramid of embroidered cushions, looking down into the flames with the satisfaction of a tyrant looking down at a burning city. His cruel eyes gleamed in the firelight. Across the room from Oba's couch, Bukhu the High Priest was walking back and forth, chewing on his knuckle. From time to time he looked as if he were about to speak, but then he would shake his head and keep walking. A servant girl, biting her lip to try to stop herself from shaking with fear, was kneeling in front of Oba and rubbing scented oil into his feet. Today the Pharaoh seemed to be in a good mood but that had not been a common sight lately.

"Sit down, Bukhu, you stalking ibis," Oba

eventually said to his High Priest. "Your constant pacing to and fro will ruin my beautiful floor."

Bukhu stopped mid-stride. "Forgive me, My Pharaoh," he said, "but am I not your most trusted advisor, and your truest friend?"

"Of course you are," Oba said. "I shall execute anyone who says otherwise."

"Well, I am troubled! This plan of yours is..." Bukhu paused, the words catching in his throat.

"Is what?" said Oba, with a slow smile that made the servant girl shudder. Silently, she wondered what his "plan" could be.

"It is reckless!" Bukhu burst out. "Reckless and foolish! Surely you can see that you are risking everything we have worked for?"

"Ah," Oba said, with mock sadness. "Perhaps I should change my mind, then, and listen to my dear old friend Bukhu, who has always been so wise."

"That would be for the best, My Pharaoh," Bukhu said with a smile.

Oba narrowed his eyes. "No, it would not!" he shouted. "I have listened to you once too often, Bukhu! Always you come up with some clever plan, and tell me the same thing! 'This time we will not fail', you say to me! 'This time we will kill Akori!' You bring me powerful Gods, like Wadjet the Cobra Goddess, Nekhbet the Vulture Goddess and Sobek the Crocodile God, claiming they will finish him! And what happens?"

Bukhu was lost for words.

Oba leaped up and kicked the bottle from the servant girl's hands. She ducked for cover as it shattered and a spray of oil flew into the fire basket. A great sheet of flame shot up. Bukhu cowered as Oba snarled at him.

"We fail every time," Oba hissed. "Wadjet

was defeated, Nekhbet was banished to the Underworld, and Sobek was turned into a baby crocodile no bigger than a newt! I took your advice, and where am I now? Worse off than when I started! The pretender to my throne has freed four of the five good Gods!"

"That is hardly my fault," Bukhu blustered. "The help he has received—"

Oba spat on the floor. "Silence. I will listen to you no more, High Priest. From now on, I make my own plans. I will not let our Dark Lord Set down."

Bukhu swallowed hard. "But the danger in your plan is so great—"

"Another word from you, and it will be your last," Oba said. "You have work to do. Get out."

Bukhu and the servant both hurried from the room.

Oba looked deep into the flames. The red light flickered in his eyes, as if he were *a demon in Oba's shape.*

"Come forth from the fire, Lord of Darkness, mighty Set," he whispered. "It is nearly time for our supreme victory! You have spoken to me many times from the smoke and the thunderclouds – now come to me in person!"

The embers trembled, heaped and spilled as a tall, dark shape began to rise from them. Two red animal eyes glared from the figure's huge head, burning more fiercely than the fire. Foul stenches filled the air. Sulphur, and the stink of wild pigs.

Oba laughed in evil delight. "Welcome, mighty Set!"

"Pharaoh," replied a voice as thick and dark as a bubbling tar pit. "What news of the pretender to your throne, Akori the farm boy? Is he dead?"

"Not yet," Oba smirked. "But he will be soon! I have a plan..."

CHAPTER ONE

The trainee priest, Manu, looked anxiously into the leaping flames.

"Do you really think this is a good idea?" he asked.

Ebe, the slave girl, looked just as nervous. Akori was sitting with his two closest friends by the great fire at the heart of the Temple of Horus. Behind them, the old High Priest sat on a chair, his frail hands clasped together. There was nobody else around to disturb them, for the other priests had all been sent away on duties. That was for their own sake as much as Akori's. What Akori was about to try could go badly wrong.

"We have to try!" Akori answered. "If Horus could still contact me on his own, he would have done so by now. I have to try to contact him."

"I say we wait a little longer," Manu said with a worried frown.

"He's not contacted me since we freed Sekhmet," Akori reminded him. "It's been almost a week. He's never been silent for this long before." Akori turned to the blind High Priest, who was nodding gravely.

"For all you know, he might appear in the next five minutes!" said Manu.

"But what if he doesn't?" Akori replied. "We can't sit and wait for ever, just *hoping*!"

Akori felt Ebe reach up to touch the falcon-shaped birthmark on his arm. Although Ebe was unable to speak, her eyes showed courage. Akori knew she was agreeing with him. He had to try and summon Horus.

Manu let out a sigh. "You're right. If Set really has broken Horus's power to reach you, then we can't bury our heads in the sand about it. I just wish it didn't have to be in the fire, that's all."

"Horus appeared in the fire last time, so it makes sense to try the fire again," Akori explained. "It might make it easier for him."

Akori remembered the last time Horus had appeared to him in the flames. The noble God had been exhausted, almost unable to speak at all. Now that the four other good Gods had been freed, passing on their magical gifts to Akori in gratitude, he was finally ready to free the leader of the good Gods, Horus himself. But how could he do that if he wasn't able to find him?

Akori took a deep breath and laid his hand on his birthmark. "Mighty Horus, Avenger, Lord of Light," he prayed, "please hear me! It is I, Akori, your Chosen One!"

Nothing happened, and Akori felt bitter disappointment creeping over him.

"See, I told you we ought to wait," Manu said, "Why don't we—"

But then, all at once, the flames rushed together, causing Manu to jump in fright. The radiant figure of a man appeared in the heart of the fire, a man with the powerful muscles of a warrior and the head of a hawk.

Akori bowed his head, Manu fell to one knee, and Ebe clapped excitedly. Horus had heard Akori's call!

But as the image grew clearer, they saw something terrible. Horus's body was hanging limp, held up by seething black energies that swirled and clutched like enchanted snakes. Horus struggled in their grasp. He lunged forward, one arm upraised, reaching out to Akori, but the living darkness held him back.

Akori, Manu and Ebe looked at one another in horror. What they had feared was true, and it was even worse than they had imagined. Horus seemed to have lost all of his power.

"My Lord!" Akori called desperately. "Tell me where to find you!"

Horus opened his beaked mouth to speak, but a writhing tentacle of darkness wound itself around his face. His words were lost.

Enraged, Akori reached for his golden *khopesh* sword, the magical gift from Horus that could cut through any material. He would slice that black tentacle in half!

But Manu placed a hand on Akori's arm to stop him. "It's only a vision, Akori – you can't help him from here!"

Horus made a fresh attempt to escape the black energies, tearing and straining with all his might, but Akori could see he was too weak. As Horus sagged back, the flames in the hearth leaped wildly for a moment, dazzling everyone.

When the flames died down again, the figure of Horus was gone. In its place was a huge snout-faced head, eyes glinting with rage.

"Oh no!" Manu cried.

Ebe let out a strange hiss of terror, and dived behind a bench.

Akori gripped his sword, feeling a deep dread in the pit of his stomach.

After all of his battles to free the good Gods, he was finally face-to-face with their captor, Set, the Lord of Darkness.

"As you can see," Set gloated, "my guest is in no condition to talk to his Chosen One." He laughed like a braying ass. "And what a

19

Chosen One you are, farm boy! You dare to challenge me, with dung and straw still in your hair?"

Akori had thought a hundred times about what he would say to Set when he finally saw him, but the sight of Set's hideous face made his throat close up in fear and he could not say a word. All at once, it seemed Set was right. He felt just like a stupid, useless farm boy, and he wanted to turn and run away without ever looking back.

Akori clenched his jaw hard. He would *not* let Set see he was scared. Reaching deep within himself, he searched for the courage he needed.

"Yes!" he yelled. "I *do* challenge you, swine-face! I beat your servants, didn't I? Every single last one! Wadjet, Am-Heh, Sobek, Heket *and* Nekhbet! And I'll beat you just the same!"

Set sneered. "You were lucky for a short time. But now your luck has run out. Run back to your fields, boy. You dare not face me."

Akori strode towards the edge of the flames, determined to answer Set's threat. He swallowed down his fear once more and looked the terrible beast-face right in the eyes. "Oh yes I do!" But his defiance had made him reckless...

"Akori, look out!" Manu yelled.

Jets of fire blasted from Set's nostrils. Akori dived to one side, avoiding the stream of flames by a whisker. Searing, painful heat reddened his arm. Ebe gave a moan.

Set's hee-hawing laughter echoed through the hall.

Fighting to keep his shock and pain hidden, Akori yelled, "Tell me where you have imprisoned Horus!"

Set laughed even harder. "Very well! If you had more wit than a dung beetle, you would have worked it out for yourself! The weakling God Horus is trapped deep within the dungeons of my own sacred place."

"The Temple of Set!" Manu whispered, obviously terrified.

"Indeed, little priest," said Set. "Though it will soon have a new name – the Tomb of the Farm Boy!"

Set roared with menacing laughter. The flames surged as if they were laughing too. Then the laughter and the image faded away together, leaving only silence.

Akori gulped as Set's words continued to echo in his ears. Was he really about to die after everything he had been through?

CHAPTER TWO

Akori's heart was beating fast and his bones felt as if they had turned to jelly. Ebe fetched a pail of water, dipped a rag in it and began wrapping it around his injured arm. It throbbed where the flame had scorched his skin but Akori didn't let the pain show. Instead, he forced out a laugh. "I can't see what everyone's so afraid of..." His voice trailed off. The High Priest was shaking his head, an expression of deep sorrow etched on his face.

"You are not speaking from the heart, Akori," he said. "Do you think your friends cannot tell? You are afraid to be afraid, and so you act brazenly. That is not wise of you."

"But I have to stand up to Set!" Akori insisted.

"Yes, but be brave, not stupid! Control your hot head!" The blind High Priest stood, shaking his staff in Akori's direction. "Set is a force of evil as old as the universe, and he is cunning! Through his trickery he was able to murder Horus's own father, Osiris – the legends have told this. You must not let him trick you into doing something reckless. Did you not see how easily he taunted you?"

"But I—"

"He provoked you into losing your temper, and nearly burned you to a cinder! If Manu had not seen what Set was trying to do and warned you in time, you would be dead now!"

"Thanks, Manu," Akori said, taking the High Priest's words to heart. "I'm sorry. I didn't think."

Manu just nodded. He was sitting white-faced, still staring at the flames where Set had been only moments before. Ebe's hands were trembling as she bandaged Akori's arm. Akori knew they were just as shaken as he was. None of them had been prepared for Set's appearance. He promised himself he would be braver than ever before. Not just for himself, but for his friends too.

"True bravery does not mean denying your fear," said the High Priest, as if he had read Akori's thoughts. "Only a fool or a madman would not be afraid in the presence of Set."

"Then...what do I do?"

"A brave man," the High Priest said simply, "is one who accepts his fear without allowing it to master him. You have to focus on what you need to do rather than worry about what might happen."

Akori nodded and tried to imagine himself freeing Horus from Set's power. He had a sudden thought. "High Priest, when the vision of Horus has appeared to us before, there have been strange black energies holding him back. Do you know what they might be?"

"Spirits of the Underworld," the High Priest replied solemnly. "Lesser demons who serve Set. They hold Horus prisoner and drain his strength, like leeches. At first, he would have been able to resist them, but even Horus does not have endless power. The weaker he becomes, the more they can feast upon him."

Akori was aghast. "Do they...hurt?"

The High Priest's face creased in sorrow.

"I will not lie to you, Akori. I believe Horus is in great pain."

The thought filled Akori with cold rage. It was bad enough imagining the mighty God Horus trapped like a broken-winged bird, but the thought of him in pain was almost too much to bear.

Manu had once told Akori how the very first Pharaoh had had to choose between Horus, who offered wisdom, and Set, who offered power. The Pharaoh had chosen Horus and rejected Set, who had been cast out. Now Set was enjoying a revenge that had been many centuries in the making. Akori clenched his fists. Well, not any more. Akori was going to put a stop to Set's evil ways once and for all.

"We're leaving for the Temple of Set as soon as we can," he announced. "Where is it, Manu?"

Manu rooted through his bag of scrolls and fished out a map. "To the north, past the great sand sea. There's a ring of huge sand dunes, big enough to be called mountains. The Temple is right in the middle."

"Is it a long journey?" Akori asked.

"The longest we've had to make," Manu replied, "and probably the hardest."

As they readied themselves for the trip, loading up on water and food, a bleak mood hung over them. Usually, there would have been excitement, jokes, and a babble of random information from Manu about this or that. But this time, although nobody was saying so out loud, Akori could tell they were all badly shaken. Set's appearance had cast a dark shadow over everything.

Akori made sure he had all of his magical

gifts. The Talisman of Ra, which could focus the power of the sun, hung round his neck. On his finger gleamed the Ring of Isis, which could make the wearer invisible. He placed the Scarab of Anubis in the pouch tied around his waist, remembering how its power to heal wounds had saved their lives before. On his left arm he bore the Shield of Sekhmet, which could deflect even the hardest blows, and would protect the bearer from evil magic. Lastly, he strapped to his belt the very first gift he'd received – the golden *khopesh* sword Horus had given him.

The High Priest blessed the three friends before they departed. Then they walked from the Temple into the bright light of day. Their journey would lead them up the course of the Nile and into desert country. There was a great distance to travel.

They headed past open fields where crops were growing, and saw ships going to and fro along the water. Although the sky was clear and the peaceful waters of the Nile glittered under the sun, the people they passed all looked nervous and scared. There was none of the usual chatter and laughter coming from the boats. There were no children playing by the water's edge. After the recent drought and flood, and the dead rising from their tombs, it was as if the whole of Egypt was waiting to see what new evil Set would unleash next.

Akori marched on. Surely if they were brave and determined enough, they could defeat this last and greatest evil?

Then, from somewhere high above, he heard a faint noise. It was the horribly familiar braying laugh of Set, very far away. Ebe grabbed Akori's arm and pointed wildly at the sky. He looked up. There in the huge gulf of clear blue sky was one sinister thundercloud, a huge gathering mass of darkness.

Akori rubbed his eyes and looked again. Storm clouds on a clear day? That wasn't possible. He had to be seeing things...

The next second, a blinding flash of lightning ripped the sky in half!

The three friends waited for the storm to break. But no rain came.

"W-what was that?" Manu stammered.

Ebe stared nervously at the sky.

Akori frowned. "I think it was a warning," he replied.

"A warning?" Manu said.

"Yes." Akori gripped his shield tightly. "From Set."

CHAPTER THREE

Many hours had passed. There had been no more lightning bolts, but the black cloud was still in the sky, spread out like a dark stain on a blue silk sheet. There was no way to deny it – the cloud was following them, and it seemed to have grown even larger.

The trio had been walking all day, with only short stops for food and water. They had left the Nile behind them long ago. Now, in the midst of the great sand sea, they were finally within sight of the mountains. They

loomed up ahead, dark against the blue sky.
Away in the west, the sun was descending
towards the horizon.

"They look like a wall," Akori said.

"In some ways, they are," said Manu. "Set
likes his temples to be in lonely places, where
only his chosen few can reach him."

"But there has to be a way in!" said Akori.
"Come on. Let's scout around and see if we
can find a path." He glanced over his shoulder.
As he had expected, the thundercloud was still
looming above them. Warily, Akori set off
across the foothills.

"Maybe things won't be so bad after all,"
Manu said as they walked.

"What makes you say that?" Akori asked
with a frown.

"We're almost at the Temple, and nothing's
tried to stop us!" Manu replied. "Every other
time we've headed out to rescue one of the

Gods, some kind of terrible beast has tried to kill us. Cobras, crocodiles, lizards...and that horrible giant hunting dog, Am-Heh. He nearly devoured all of us!"

Akori glanced up at the black cloud. It seemed to be getting closer. He shook his head and kept walking. No matter what Manu said, he knew they weren't going to have it easy. Set was not going to give up Horus without a fight.

The sun was nearly at the horizon, and though they had trudged for hours they had still found no way through the mountains. Struggling across the dunes was hard work and they were making little progress.

"I have to rest soon," Manu groaned, squinting up at the looming wall of sand. "I can't go on like this!"

Ebe nodded. Her hair was plastered to

her forehead with sweat.

"We have to keep going!" Akori said. "We can't be caught out here when night falls. Who knows what could come looking for us this close to the Temple of Set?"

"You think we'll be any safer *inside* the Temple?" grumbled Manu. He was about to walk on when Akori stopped him.

"Wait," Akori said. "Maybe we do need to rest. What's the use in arriving at the Temple if we're too exhausted to fight? We'll stop for some water and then press on."

They sat down, grateful for the chance to rest their aching feet. As Manu passed the waterskins around, Akori looked up at the setting sun to see how much daylight they had left.

A dark shape moved across the horizon. Akori squinted and saw that it was a rider on a horse, only a dozen paces away!

Startled, he leaped to his feet and yelled, brandishing his sword at the figure. How had he not heard them coming?

"Peace be with you, young ones!" called a gentle female voice. "Put down your sword. We mean you no harm."

The rider approached, and Akori saw that there was a second rider behind her. Both were hooded women with long flowing cloaks. Their saddles were hung with hundreds of silver coins threaded together. There was a strange, unearthly beauty about the women. Their lips were full, their features proud and regal. Their dark skin glimmered with rich cosmetics, so they had to be very wealthy. Akori thought they might be high Egyptian nobility – princesses, maybe, or even queens.

Manu and Ebe scrambled to their feet as the women approached.

"Who are you?" Akori shouted. He wasn't putting his sword away just yet, he decided.

The woman in front halted her horse and smiled. Her skin glittered with powdered gold, and her eyes were a deep dark blue. Akori stared at her, suspicious but still amazed. She was more beautiful than any woman he had ever seen in his life.

"We are travellers like yourselves!" she answered. "We ride from Heliopolis, the City of the Sun."

"And you?" said the second rider, who had halted alongside. She was just as beautiful as her companion. Her eyes were green and her skin sparkled with silver. "This is a lonely place for three children to be out wandering."

"We are not children, and our business is our own," Akori said gruffly.

"Akori!" said Manu, shocked. "Where are your manners?"

But the women just laughed in a friendly way, as if Akori had made a joke.

"We do not blame you for being cautious!" said the blue-eyed one. "The desert is a strange and haunted place, especially after dark. It is wise to be wary."

Akori glanced up at the sky. The sinister cloud was still above them – bigger and blacker than ever.

"And travellers must look out for one another," said the woman with green eyes. "That is the custom in the desert. Come, can we not offer you a ride? Your feet look sore, and we do not mind walking for a while."

"Well, my feet are very sore," Manu began. "What do you say, Akori?"

Akori glanced at Ebe. She still looked very tired. At least if they got a ride they would have more energy to fight. "All right," he said warily.

"We're heading for the Temple of Set, and we need to get there as quickly as we can," Manu said to the women.

"Climb aboard!" they replied, and gracefully dismounted. The horses were huge elegant beasts, covered in glossy black hair, but they snuffled in a friendly way as the trio approached. Ebe reached up to stroke one of them on the nose.

Akori climbed onto the lead horse, while Manu and Ebe clambered onto the other. Soon they were trotting briskly across the sand, with the women striding alongside.

"This beats walking, eh, Akori?" Manu called out.

Akori remained silent. He was glad to be off his feet, but he felt that something wasn't quite right. The women hadn't reacted at all when Manu said they were going to the Temple of Set. Surely any right-minded desert traveller would at least *shudder* when you spoke of Set? He was the most evil of all the Gods. Either the women didn't know this...or they had no reason to fear him. The second possibility bothered him most.

Before long, they found the long-awaited entrance to the ring of sandy mountains. A narrow pass lay between two of the huge peaks, gaping like a hungry mouth. The women guided the horses down into the deepening shadow. With every step the horses took, Akori felt more and more anxious. Why were the women not afraid?

There was hardly any light now. The mountains blotted out what little sun there was, so that they were riding into almost total darkness. Akori tightened his grip on the leather saddle. He was sure they were being watched. On the rocky walls to either side, the shadows seemed to be moving. Out of the corner of his eye, Akori thought he saw a deformed, inhuman head peer at him as he went by. When he glanced at it, it vanished.

Without warning, they emerged from the other end of the mountain pass. They had arrived in an open area like a great crater in the midst of the mountains. There in the centre loomed a jagged black structure. It had five towers, and looked strangely like a clawed hand clutching up from the earth. The Temple of Set!

"Almost there now!" Manu called out to Akori. "Nice to travel in style for once, isn't it? Makes the journey fly past!"

The woman down below Akori looked over her shoulder. But she wasn't looking at Akori. She was looking up at the sky, and she was smiling – a horrible, sinister smile.

Akori followed her gaze with horror.

Directly above them, the black cloud that had been following them for the entire journey still hovered. Only it wasn't a shapeless cloud any more. It had formed into the shape of a snout-faced beast, the ears long, the deep eyes crackling with red lightning. Akori had seen that face before, glaring at him out of the fire. It was the face of Set!

The echo of braying laughter resounded round the valley, closer and louder now. The blue-eyed woman turned to her companion and nodded.

The green-eyed woman reached up and pulled back her hood. Akori stared at her in disbelief. Sprouting from her forehead were two long, curved horns!

CHAPTER FOUR

The horned woman grinned, showing sharp, leopard-like teeth. Behind her on his horse, completely unaware of what was going on, Manu was shouting enthusiastically.

"We've reached the Temple already!" he cried, leaning gratefully against the horse's neck. "Thank you so much for bringing us here, it was so kind of—"

"Manu!" Akori yelled. "They're not what they seem! Look!"

Before Manu had a chance to react, the

horned woman shouted some strange harsh-sounding words to the horses.

Immediately the horses started to rear up and neigh, bucking wildly. Steam hissed from their huge nostrils, steam that smelled fouler than rotting flesh. Manu nearly went flying. Ebe grabbed fistfuls of mane and clung on tight. The creature bellowed in pain. Manu caught Ebe around the waist and managed to stay on the horse's back – just.

Akori desperately hung on to his saddle. The horse bucked and tossed like a ship in a storm, snorting and thrashing this way and that. Akori tried to see what the sinister women were doing, but it was hard enough just staying on the horse's back. One thing he knew for sure was that there was going to be a fight, and he had to arm himself!

Gripping the saddle with his legs, he clutched the Shield of Sekhmet in one hand

and drew his golden *khopesh* sword with the other. Just then, the horse reared like a striking snake. Akori lost his grip on his *khopesh* and it went flying end over end, landing somewhere in the sand behind him.

The women were removing their hoods and cloaks now, and Akori could see their faces changing in the half-light. Their chins lengthened and became pointed. Their cheeks grew hollow and their eyes turned into long narrow slits. They hissed and snarled, licking their lips. Beneath their robes, they wore battle armour made of polished leather. Each one carried a matching spear, long and slender with a gleaming knife-like tip.

"Time to die!" hissed the nearest one, hurling her spear right at Akori as if she were spearing a fish!

He only had one chance. He let go of the

saddle and leaned backwards out of the way. The spear went whistling past, almost grazing his chest.

The woman-creature clicked her tongue angrily, and the spear was suddenly in her hand again.

Akori tried to regain his grip on the saddle, but the horse could feel he was loose and bucked hard. He felt himself flying through the air, then he landed with an agonizing *whump* on the ground.

His side ached, but he couldn't help that now. If he stayed there he was a sitting target. Those spears would be through his ribs in seconds. He fought to sit up – and then everything was plunged into darkness.

Akori stumbled to his feet. He could barely see a thing. He knew he hadn't gone blind, because he could just make out the outline of the horse looming over him. But why was it suddenly as black as midnight? Was this some kind of sorcery? And what had happened to Manu and Ebe?

Akori looked up and saw a thick layer of darkness above him glimmering with lightning. In a flash he understood. The black cloud that had been following them all day had come down out of the sky. Now it was completely covering the hollow in the middle of the ring of mountains. It was like a lid on a pot, blocking out all the sunlight.

Somewhere in the darkness, Manu cried out. There was a thump, followed by another. He and Ebe must have been thrown from their horse, like Akori had been. He had to move fast. He could see the demonic women now, standing out darkly like silhouettes, their spears raised. They were closing in on Manu and Ebe!

First he had to find his *khopesh*. Akori

looked around, peering through the darkness, trying to see where it had landed. A glimmer of lightning from above gave a split second of light – just enough for Akori to see his precious sword gleaming from the side of a dune. He ran and snatched it up.

When he turned back he could see shadowy figures flailing about in the darkness. The women snarled and hissed while the horses snorted and stamped. Manu yelled and Ebe screamed as they tried to fight them off.

Akori moved closer, *khopesh* and shield at the ready, every muscle tense.

"We've been tricked!" Manu wailed. "I know who they are."

Akori said nothing. He didn't want to give his position away. If the women didn't know where he was, he'd have the benefit of surprise.

"They're two of Set's wives!" Manu yelled. "Anat and Astarte, the warrior Goddesses!"

"And you," hissed a cruel voice, "are our prey."

"And our prey," another voice growled, "never escapes alive!"

The women suddenly spun away from Manu and Ebe and came racing towards Akori. They had known he was there all along! A spear came whirring out of the darkness, aimed at his heart.

Akori raised the Shield of Sekhmet just in time. The spear struck it with full force and shattered into splinters.

He heard Anat scream in rage. "My war-spear! You will pay for that!"

She came charging at him, panting heavily, her head lowered, her sharp horns ready to impale him. Akori stood braced to meet her charge. As she thrust her horns at him,

Akori ran and leaped into the air, flipped head over heels and landed behind her. With a yell he spun around and hacked at Anat's side. The blade of his *khopesh* bit deep into her armour and she howled in pain. But now Astarte was flanking him, readying her own spear. Akori tensed, as if he were getting ready to leap again. Astarte grinned. She threw the spear – but Akori ducked instead of jumping and the spear flew high over his head. If he'd leaped, it would have pierced right through his stomach and out the other side. Astarte gave a cheated snarl.

Still hissing and clutching her wound, Anat retreated into the darkness, leaving Akori to face Astarte. Akori felt a brief flash of triumph. Astarte was a terrifying foe, but at least she was now alone.

Astarte began running at him, gripping her spear with both hands, its point aimed at his

chest. Akori raised the Shield of Sekhmet, more grateful than ever for its protection now he had seen what it could do. But at the last minute, Astarte dug the spear point into the sand like a pole vault. The long spear flexed, and she came flying through the air at him!

Akori covered himself with the shield just in time. Astarte landed on him with a tremendous crash, knocking him to the ground. She loomed over him, her horned image even darker than the storm cloud above. Akori rolled aside as her spear stabbed down at him again and again.

Thinking fast, he quickly twisted the Ring of Isis and vanished, becoming invisible. Then he rolled over and over until he was well out of spear range. He heard Astarte cursing and lunging randomly at the sand, trying to find him.

Scrambling to his feet, he ran into the dark. He had to find Manu and Ebe and get them out of there before it was too late! But how could he guide them if they couldn't see him? He twisted the ring again and became visible.

A flash of lightning lit up the whole region. Akori saw Manu less than a spear's throw away. His face was frozen in panic and his hands were raised as if to ward off something terrible. The next moment, Akori saw Anat charging at his friend. Akori gave a cry and began to run to Manu's aid, but it was hopeless. More lightning lit up the deadly scene. Manu cowered...Anat's horns struck...they speared through Manu's body. She flung him upward like a bull tossing a victim.

Darkness fell once again, as Manu screamed a long, dying scream of agony.

Akori had to drive back the darkness. He fumbled for the Talisman of Ra around his neck and began a desperate prayer. "Mighty Ra, God of the Sun," he began, "send us your—"

Before he could say any more, a blood-chilling roar echoed through the valley. It sounded like a lion, though surely no mortal lion could ever make such a sound. Then he saw it, leaping out of the darkness – the huge, tawny shape of a monstrous cat-like beast, growling in savage hunger.

It was running straight for Manu's crumpled body!

CHAPTER FIVE

The lion-beast's growling ripped through the darkness again and again. Akori knew Manu had no chance. It would tear him to pieces – unless Akori could stop it in time. He ran as hard as he could, *khopesh* drawn and ready. Whatever the beast was, he would not stand back and let it make a meal of his fallen friend. It would have to look somewhere else for its meat, the filthy scavenger. He would fight it to his dying breath...

As he reached Manu, Akori's anger gave

way to confusion. The lion-beast was not there. He stood over Manu, ready to defend him, but nothing happened. Manu's only wounds were where Anat's horns had gored him. But Akori could still hear furious snarls and growls. What was going on? He peered into the darkness. There was the lion-beast, running *away* from Manu. It was chasing something, a fleeing horned figure that ran with a strange lope. It was Anat!

Akori rubbed his eyes and stared harder into the darkness. It was true. The creature was chasing the demon away. She was scrambling to escape as fast as she could! A terrible scream rang out as the lion-beast gained on her.

Akori had to get a better view. He grasped the Talisman of Ra and held it high above his head, praying, "Mighty Ra, God of the Sun, send us your aid!"

59

Light began pouring out from the talisman. The valley was lit up as bright as day, but for the heavy curtain of black cloud above them. The warrior Goddesses were now small figures in the distance. The two horses were bolting with them. Akori watched the evil group run, and soon the sandy mountains had swallowed them up. As for the lion-beast, it was nowhere to be seen.

Akori hung the dazzling amulet back around his neck, where it glowed like a second burning heart. Then he turned back to Manu. His friend was clutching his belly and moaning, his fingers covered in blood. Ebe was bent over him now, doing her best to make him comfortable.

Akori kneeled at Manu's side. His thoughts flashed back to the last time Manu had been wounded. The healing Scarab of Anubis had saved his life then, but would it still work now? Akori tugged it from his pouch so hastily he tore the cloth. Manu was trembling like a dog with a broken leg. There was blood on his mouth as well as his stomach. Ebe looked as if she were about to cry.

Manu had clearly lost a lot of blood. Akori had the sudden, shocking feeling that he had left it too late. He should have tended to Manu immediately, instead of watching the Goddesses.

Akori held the scarab pin to the wound. "Lord Anubis," he prayed, "heal our friend!" Although he didn't say it out loud, he thought to himself: *It'll be my fault if he dies and I couldn't bear it...*

The scarab twitched to life and scuttled across Manu. He winced as it went to work.

To Akori's amazement, Manu's wound began to fade and disappear.

"It's working!" he said, and the relief he felt was sweeter than all the honey in Heliopolis.

Manu coughed and began to breathe a little more easily, his eyes fixing on Akori. "Did you see it?" he gasped. "Huge...wild cat! It helped me. Fought...Anat...off."

"I saw!" Akori said. "I'm glad it was on our side, but what was it?"

"M-must have been Sekhmet," Manu said. He still looked very pale. "In lioness form. She helped us before."

"It couldn't have been!" said Akori firmly. "Why would Sekhmet have come? It doesn't make sense. I didn't call to her. Besides, that wild cat was much smaller than Sekhmet in her lioness form. Don't you remember when she carried us back to the Temple of Horus?"

"All three of us rode on her back," said Manu, smiling at the memory.

"With room to spare," Akori added. "I don't think that thing could have carried more than one of us! Anyway, you're alive. That's the important thing."

Akori looked at Ebe, who was giving Manu a drink of water. He wished she could speak. Perhaps she could tell him where the cat-thing had come from.

At that moment, Akori's birthmark tingled, reminding him of his quest. "Ebe, you stay here with Manu," he said. "I need to get inside the Temple of Set and find Horus."

Ebe nodded gravely and curled her hand into a fist. She mimed punching at imaginary things that were menacing Manu.

Akori smiled. "No, you won't have to fight anything! Here." He pulled the Ring of Isis from his finger and passed it to her. "This will keep you safe. You can make yourselves invisible."

Ebe seemed pleased by that, but Manu angrily tried to sit up. "You're not going anywhere without us!" he said.

"Yes I am. Stay here and rest."

"I'm fine!" said Manu, standing up. He wobbled unsteadily, then sank to his knees again. "I'm just a little dizzy."

Akori shook his head. "I'm sorry, Manu. The Scarab of Anubis may have saved your life, but you've still lost a lot of blood. You're in no condition to walk, let alone fight. Especially not against any more of Set's minions!"

"You should be worrying about yourself, not me," Manu said. "Going into the Temple of Set alone? You've always had us with you before."

"I don't think I've got any choice," Akori said seriously. He turned to look towards the temple. "This is my destiny. Everything that's happened so far has led us here, to this moment. It's all happened for a reason."

Manu frowned. "Are you saying that we aren't *meant* to follow you inside the temple?"

Akori nodded as the realization dawned upon him. "The Prophecy of the Sphinx says the fate of Egypt rests on my shoulders, and mine alone. That means I have to confront Set on my own. It's the path I have to follow, laid down thousands of years before any of us were born. None of us can change it."

"Very well," Manu sighed. "Go and meet your destiny. But prophecy or no prophecy, if I've got my strength back before you come out of there alive and well, I'm going in after you!" Ebe nodded vigorously in agreement.

Akori smiled at them gratefully. It might have been his destiny to face Set alone, but he would never have got to this point if it hadn't been for the bravery and support of his friends. Akori's smile faded as he thought of the challenge that lay ahead of him. Set would be his most deadly foe yet. What if he didn't make it back out of the temple alive? Would this be the last time he ever saw Manu and Ebe? As if reading his mind, Manu grasped hold of Akori's arm.

"Be careful," he whispered.

Ebe gripped Akori's arm and nodded her own message of support.

"Thank you," Akori said, "for everything."

Then he stood up and set off into the darkness. The temple stood before him, its blackened towers like monuments to all the dark Gods who had ever been. From openings in the towers, reddish vapours seethed, with hideous faces appearing in them like tormented ghosts. This was the heart of Set's power on earth, like a furnace where pure evil was forged. It was where Set must have come when the very first Pharaoh rejected his offer of allegiance, to brood and make his dark plans for revenge. Beneath Akori's feet the ground felt hot, as if Set's fiery underworld were right here, waiting to devour him.

Akori wished more than anything that he could just turn back time, to when he was nothing more than a simple farm boy dreaming in the sun by the flowing Nile. Life was so much simpler then, before he knew his true destiny.

He forced himself to walk on. Even if it led to his death, he must follow his fate. It had led him to all of the other good Gods, hadn't it?

As he walked, Akori felt his birthmark begin to tingle again. That was the sign of his royal blood, marking him as the true Pharaoh – if he survived long enough to take the throne. It reminded him that he was the heir of that very first Pharaoh, the one who had found the strength to defy Set. Akori prayed that he would have that same strength now as he walked on, deeper into the darkness.

CHAPTER SIX

Back in the Temple of Horus, Akori had seen a picture of a dead man's soul in the Underworld. Manu had explained it to him. The man was approaching a gateway, while monstrous beasts watched from all around. He would have to walk through the gates alone and confront the horrors that waited there. Only then could he pass on into eternal life. If he failed, he would be devoured and lost for ever. The memory of the picture came back to Akori now as he made his way to the entrance of Set's temple. He was all alone in the darkness, approaching the gate that led inside. And there was no telling what hungry evils were waiting there.

The pillars of the great gate were carved from black rock. Giant sphinxes flanked it, but they had smooth featureless ovals instead of faces. Above the gate stood a statue of Set in all his terrible glory, holding the limp body of Horus in one hand and trampling the body of Osiris beneath his feet. As Akori approached, the statue's eyes filled with a red glow and steam hissed from the nostrils. Taking a deep breath, Akori drew his *khopesh* and walked in.

The corridors were dark and stifling hot. A foul-smelling breeze was blowing from somewhere. The only light came from the Talisman of Ra, still dimly glowing around Akori's neck. He considered calling on its

power to light his way more clearly, then changed his mind. He would save its power for later, when he might need it more.

Akori glanced at the paintings on the walls as he ventured further into the temple. They showed terrible scenes of battle and death. What made it worse were the familiar figures in the pictures. There was Am-Heh, the ferocious Hunter God, a limp victim hanging from his jaws. Wadjet the Snake Goddess was coiled around a group of helpless people, as if she were about to crush them all at once. Sobek the Crocodile God was leering down at a pit full of prisoners, while his frog-headed wife squatted beside him.

"You don't scare me, any of you," Akori whispered to the pictures. "I beat you all." Although what he said was true, his words somehow sounded hollow, like the boast of a fool.

Akori clutched his *khopesh* and shield and moved further down the empty, silent corridor. Set had said Horus was in the dungeon, but Akori had no idea how to get to it. Up ahead, a single torch was flickering. Akori headed for it, passing dozens of animal-headed statues on the way. He recognized none of them. Could they all be allies of Set? Were there really that many evil Gods? He half expected them to lurch into life, cold stone hands clutching for him...but they stayed still and silent.

When he got to the torch he saw a door in the wall. He reached to push it open, then hesitated. Every nerve in Akori's body sang out a warning. Why were there no guards? Such an important temple must surely have some. Was Set trying to trick him into doing something reckless and foolish? It would not be the first time...

Slowly, with great care, Akori pushed open the door. He blinked, suddenly dazzled, and rubbed his eyes. The passageway ahead was lined with hundreds of flickering torches. And there in front of him, his sword and shield shining in the torchlight, was a young boy of Akori's age. Despite his youth, he looked lean and muscular. There was a wild look in his eye, as if he were braced to attack. Akori caught his breath. Only one boy could possibly be waiting to fight him here in Set's temple. His rival, the evil Pharaoh Oba!

Akori raised his *khopesh* and prepared to charge. The boy did the same. His *khopesh* was the twin of Akori's own. It was even the same gold colour.

Akori stopped. The boy stopped too. Slowly Akori raised his hand. When the boy imitated him, he realized the truth. This was not Oba at all. It was his own reflection.

Now he looked more closely at the walls, he could see they were all made from highly polished metal.

Akori wondered how he could have made such a silly mistake, and then he looked at himself again. He hadn't seen his reflection in a long time, and he had changed. The challenges and trials of his many journeys had toughened him. When he first set out on this quest to free the good Gods, he had been a boy. Now he seemed to have become a young man – a warrior. No wonder he hadn't recognized himself.

From somewhere close, an inhuman cackle rang out. Akori recognized it immediately as Set. So, he was not alone in this place after all. Warily, he advanced. Every so often there would be a gap in the wall leading to another, identical passageway. Before long, he realized that he had stepped inside a labyrinth. The reflective walls made it almost impossible to tell which way he was going. It was hard to work out where the open spaces were. Sometimes he misjudged and bumped painfully into a wall. He soon decided to put his *khopesh* back into his belt and feel his way ahead.

In some places there were torches flickering all around, and their reflections multiplied hundreds of times gave the effect of endless tunnels into infinity. It was making Akori's head spin. In others, the darkness was almost complete, so he had to grope through it, his heartbeat hammering in his ears.

He forced himself to concentrate. Once, when they were exploring the catacombs under the Temple of Horus, Manu had told him the trick to working your way through a labyrinth – always keep your right hand against a wall, and that way you will come to the centre eventually. Breathing evenly to calm his nerves, he pressed on.

After some minutes, Akori felt he had to be making progress. He had to be getting close to the dungeon by now, surely. But then he saw something that made him stop dead in his tracks.

Up ahead was a stretch of shadow where no torches shone. But there was a light there. It was livid and red, shining from two slitted eyes that hovered in the dark!

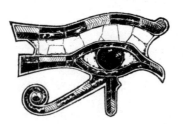

CHAPTER SEVEN

Akori drew his *khopesh* and charged. He swept the heavy blade around as he ran, meaning to slice the unseen creature's head off in one blow. Next second he crashed into a wall. He went staggering back, shocked and winded. The pain made his ears ring. And the eyes were still there. That meant they had to be a reflection. So whatever owned those eyes was lurking behind him...

Akori spun around. There were the eyes, glaring at him out of the dark. With renewed confidence and rising anger, he charged again. Set's laughter echoed through the maze as Akori slammed into another wall. He spun around again, confused. How was that possible? There had to be some kind of sorcery at work.

The eyes seemed to be all around him. Akori lashed out blindly, striking against the walls with his *khopesh*. He had to reach Horus to free him, but there seemed to be no way out of this madhouse!

He felt something brush against his back. Instantly, he turned to see the ghoulish eyes staring right at him. They were burning like balls of fire.

He bit back a scream. The thing was only a few paces away. Akori had never seen anything like it, even in Manu's most ancient scrolls. It was skeletal, wearing the tattered remains of a robe, but the head where the eyes burned was like the horned skull of an antelope. Bony fingers clutched a huge wooden sickle with a sharp flint blade.

The thing gave a ghastly shriek of victory. It raised the sickle, ready to hew Akori in half. Akori backed off along the passageway, his sword and the shield trembling in his hands. The skeletal thing cocked its head, as if it were amused by this game of cat and mouse. Then it flung its jaws open and a plume of fire came roaring out.

Akori turned and started to run. He barely outran the blast. The fiery breath was hot on his back, and he could smell his own hair burning. Frantically, he searched for a gap in the wall. He found one and slipped through. He emerged into yet another corridor of mirrors. No time to curse his luck – he had to keep moving. He raced along the passageway, his endless mirrored reflections running alongside. Then he stopped. The flaming eyes were in front of him once again, and they were coming steadily towards him!

"It's not possible!" Akori gasped. "How could it do that?"

As if in answer, Set's beast-like laugh rang in his ears. The creature was close now, so very close.

As the terrible burning eyes bore down upon him, Akori wished he still had the Ring of Isis. If he'd ever needed to be invisible, now was the time! There was nothing for it but to fight. He readied himself to charge. Then the High Priest's words came back to him: "Control your hot head! You must not let him trick you into doing something reckless..."

The skeletal thing was almost upon him. The razor-sharp sickle was drawing back for the killing blow. Akori waited, holding his breath. It seemed to be in front of him, but he had been fooled before. He let out all his breath in one great battle cry, and stepped forwards as if he was going to charge. Then, at the very last second, he spun around, and thrust.

A terrible roar echoed through the labyrinth. The *khopesh* grated against ancient bone. It was buried to the hilt in the creature's body. It had been behind him after all!

Akori ripped the *khopesh* free, sending the creature staggering. Whatever it was, he had hurt it – though he wasn't sure how he was going to kill something that seemed to have been dead for centuries.

Screeching in fury, the creature swung its sickle. Akori sidestepped the first blow and parried the second. He made a swift counter-attack, smashing his sword hard against the

84

thing's face. The jaw shattered on one side
and hung lopsided. Teeth went rattling across
the floor. But that just seemed to make it
angrier. Flinging its arms wide, it breathed
a stream of fire. Akori pressed himself flat
against the wall, only just avoiding it.

They traded furious blows. Every slice
and stab that Akori made, the creature
knocked aside with its own weapon. When
Akori's attacks began to falter, it fought back
with terrible strength. One mighty two-
handed stroke nearly took his head off, but he
ducked and the blow smashed into the
mirrored wall.

Akori had to finish this somehow. He tried
a surprise swipe at the thing's legs, but his
blade just passed through smoky nothingness.
To his horror he saw that it *had* no legs, and
was hanging in the air like a spirit. No
wonder it had moved so silently. Changing

tactics, the creature began to spin the sickle in its hands, whirling it faster and faster. Akori had no choice but to back away from it as it glided towards him. If he approached that spinning blade, he'd be sliced to pieces! The only thing to do was back slowly down the corridor. Making a shrill noise that might have been laughter, the creature advanced on him. Akori retreated a step and suddenly felt a cold, hard surface against his back.

All too late, he understood why the creature had laughed. It had backed him into a dead end. It was closing in, and there was nowhere left for him to run.

Cackling in evil glee, the creature craned its head forward. Fire was welling up between its shattered jaws, growing fierce and bright. Akori was sure it was readying a fireball that would blast him to ash. If he attacked now, he'd be burned up in seconds! But there was no cover and nowhere to run.

Then he remembered his shield's other powers. When Sekhmet had given it to him, she had said that it wasn't just for protection against weapons – it was a defence against evil magic, too. It was his only chance. He held the shield before him. "Sekhmet, Queen of Battles, hear me now!" he prayed. "Grant me your protection!"

The creature's jaws were opening. Fire danced within, reflected in hundreds of mirrors to either side. Holding his shield high and yelling at the top of his voice, Akori charged. The creature breathed out a tremendous blast of fire. Akori felt the shield thrumming on his arm as it took the full force of the blast.

A burning gale blew past him. Flames curled around the shield's rim. He yelled again, fighting to hold the shield steady as the blast threatened to tear it from his hands. For a second he was sure he would lose his grip and the flames would engulf him. But then the shield began to glow with an uncanny blue light. Akori felt the jet of fire slacken, then explode back out of the shield! He peered over the edge. To his amazement, the shield was reflecting the flames back down the corridor. It had to be Sekhmet's magic!

The creature was floating in the midst of the corridor, arms spread, staring aghast at the immense wall of fire that rushed back at it. It flung its arms over its face, trying to ward the flames off, but there was no escape.

A terrible howl rang out as the creature was consumed by its own roaring fire.

The black robe burned up like a scrap of filthy rag. The bones popped and split like dry sticks in a fire. Screeching, the skull whipped back and forth, the jaw flying loose. Then the screech stopped suddenly as the skull exploded into a thousand flaming fragments. Eventually, the flames died down, leaving a pile of smouldering ashes in the corridor.

Akori poked the heap of cinders and bone with his *khopesh*. There was no movement. The ancient nightmare was dead at last. He murmured a prayer of thanks to Sekhmet. If he ever got out of there alive, he would make the biggest offering of fresh fish her temple cats had ever seen. Watching the darkness carefully in case any more underworld demons came surging out of it, he progressed deeper into the labyrinth.

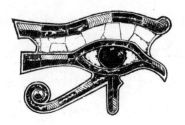

CHAPTER EIGHT

The mirrored corridors twisted and turned
but seemed to lead round in endless circles.
In the frenzy of the fight, Akori had lost
track of which wall he was touching and
couldn't use Manu's method any more. Time
after time, he found himself back at the heap
of smoking remains. He was growing
frustrated and desperate. His arm kept
tingling, probably from where the creature's
fire had singed him, and he rubbed it in
irritation. Where was the dungeon? It had to

be at the heart of this endless maze. But there was no clue anywhere to be seen. All the mirrored panels looked the same.

Akori sank against the wall and closed his eyes, exhausted. If only Horus could somehow send him a sign. He was so close, and the maddening tingle in his arm just wouldn't stop.

Akori opened his eyes and stared at his arm. Of course – how had he not understood before? His arm wasn't tingling from the flames. It was his birthmark! He and Horus were connected, and the falcon-shaped birthmark was the key. It must be reacting to the God's presence. The closer he came to Horus, the stronger the feeling became!

Akori moved down the corridor, feeling the tingle grow stronger. It was leading him to Horus, as surely as a compass points north. Halfway along the corridor, his arm

suddenly felt as if it were on fire. He stopped.
The entrance to the dungeon had to be right
in front of him, but there was nothing to be
seen except identical mirrored panels. For a
moment he wondered if he'd imagined the
telltale tingling. Was it all a trick? No. Horus
had to be here.

Akori pushed the panel in front of him,
and it slid inwards slightly. It was a
concealed door! Stone steps led downwards –
he had found the entrance to the dungeon at
last. He descended, shield and sword at the
ready. From up ahead came a faint light.

The dungeon was a circular room like
the bottom of a huge well. There were no
torches. The light was shining from the
sprawled figure of Horus, who lay
spreadeagled on the stone floor. His
whole body was glowing dimly, like the
last embers of a dying fire. Writhing black

energies bound him hand and foot.

Akori ran to his side, overjoyed to have found his God at last, but dreading that he might be too late.

Horus's hawk head lay still, his eyes closed. The demonic bindings had drained him dry and he was unconscious, his life force almost gone. Back in the temple, Akori had yearned to take his sword to those black manacles of energy, but then they had only been a vision. Now they were real, and it was time to fulfil his destiny. He had to free Horus!

Akori stood by Horus's huge wrist, where a thick band of pulsing darkness bound him. He raised his *khopesh* and brought it slashing down. The sword rebounded. The energies beneath writhed like leeches, but seemed as strong and thick as ever.

"No!" Akori shouted. He hacked again,

once, twice, like a butcher chopping at a leg of meat. Every time, the sword bounced off. Unharmed, the energies seethed and circled. Akori struck at Horus's bonds furiously but he could not harm them at all. He roared in frustration. This was not how it was supposed to be. He was too late after all. They had absorbed too much of Horus's strength.

Then an idea began forming in his mind. Maybe he could find a way to restore the God's strength. He took the scarab pin from his pouch and placed it on Horus's chest. "Great Anubis, I call on you once more," he prayed. "Horus himself needs your aid!"

The scarab sprang to life. It seemed to know exactly what to do, scuttling underneath the closest of the black bonds.

For a moment, nothing happened. Then Horus's huge limbs began to stir. The scarab scurried across his body, vanishing underneath another bond. Akori watched, holding his breath in his excitement. It was feeding life back into his veins!

Horus's eyes flickered open. He looked at Akori, and the corners of his mouth twitched in a smile. He tried to lift his arm, but the black energies dragged it back down. They were still too strong. Akori tried to think of a way to weaken them. As they were powers of darkness, maybe he could fight them with light.

He grabbed the Talisman of Ra and pointed it at the black energies binding Horus's wrist. "Ra, God of the Sun," he prayed, "send me your light!"

A brilliant beam of light shone out of the talisman. It struck the black energies and a sizzling hiss echoed around the dungeon. The energies shrivelled, eaten away by the sunlight like rusty metal dissolving in acid.

There was an agonized squeal, high and inhuman, like a wild pig caught in a trap. Using one hand to keep the sunbeam trained on the blackness, Akori drew his *khopesh* with the other. He struck at the spot where the energy seemed weakest, and this time there was a violent crunch, as if he were hacking at old blackened wood. He'd hurt it! Encouraged, he struck again, while Horus strained at his bonds, stretching them to breaking point, fighting to be free. Akori gave a yell and struck yet again.

The bond suddenly broke. Horus sat up with a triumphant roar, his arm free. He tore the remaining energies from his hands and feet, grasping them like handfuls of writhing snakes and hurling them away. Then he stood up, a fierce golden light shining from his eyes. It was matched by the gold glow now radiating from Akori's birthmark.

The energies swirled angrily around the room, screeching. Akori remembered what the High Priest had said – they were not just bonds, but demons. They started gathering around him. Akori saw greedy, sucker-like mouths open in their shadowy bodies. He had much less life force than a God. They would take only seconds to drain his life away. He raised the Shield of Sekhmet just as the first of the ropy black things struck. It rebounded harmlessly off the shield. Next moment, the glowing hand of Horus had snatched it up.

The God looked down with contempt at the struggling dark thing. "Your feasting days are over," he said.

Akori watched in awe as he tore it in half with his sharp beak. With vengeful fury, he grabbed all the others and ripped them to bits. When the last of the demons had been destroyed, Horus laid a grateful hand on Akori's shoulder.

"My debt to you is greater than any words can say," he said in a low, deep voice. "I was right to trust you. You have repaid that trust a thousand times over. Come. Let us leave this place."

Gratefully, Akori turned to leave. *It's over at last*, he thought. *And we've won! I can't wait to tell Ebe and Manu!* But then he froze. Something was descending the dungeon stairs. It was a terrible figure, muscular and blackish-red, with eyes like pits of molten hate. Akori took a step back. His legs had gone suddenly weak. He knew that long face, those wide nostrils, those bared mule-like teeth. This was no vision in the smoke. This was reality. He was face-to-face with Set himself!

CHAPTER NINE

"Did you really think it would be that easy, farm boy?" Set mocked. "I think you need to be taught a harsh lesson." From behind his back he drew two curved swords, holding one in each hand. They were like giant versions of Akori's own *khopesh*, but instead of gleaming gold, they were blood red. Set scraped the blades together like an executioner sharpening a knife and grinned horribly. Hot sparks flew at Akori's face and his heart was pounding so hard it hurt, but he stood his ground.

"You are too late!" Horus roared, moving to stand between Set and Akori. "I am free!"

"Imprisoning you was a mistake," snarled Set. "I should have murdered you just like I murdered Osiris, your father!"

Horus and Akori looked at each other. With one voice, they roared a war cry and leaped into the attack.

Set's first blow slammed against the Shield of Sekhmet with the force of a toppling oak tree. He let out a gloating laugh. The laughter soon stopped as he saw Akori had not only stayed on his feet, but was coming back at him just as hard. The *khopesh* screamed through the air in a downward slash so fierce Set had to bring both of his blades up to parry it.

Horus had no weapons but he did not need any. He dealt Set a vicious blow. Set staggered, grunted, recovered himself and began to fight in earnest.

There was no grace in Set's fighting. He used nothing but brute force. Blow after blow rained down on Akori, who dodged and weaved out of the way. Stone chips flew up from the floor where the blades struck.

Set roared in anger. He was gigantic, stronger than an army – but Akori was smaller and faster and he had had plenty of practice fighting the other Gods. Whenever Set was able to land a blow, the Shield of Sekhmet was there, turning the blow aside. Horus himself launched strike after strike, pummelling Set and slowly wearing him down.

Set's fury was growing. In a sudden vicious move, he threw one blade at Akori and the other at Horus, who dodged. Akori deflected Set's flying blade, narrowly escaping being cut in half. The sword embedded itself in the wall behind him.

Akori gritted his teeth, forcing his fear down. Now was his chance! He risked a wild slash and gored Set in the leg.

With a grunt of surprise, Set fell to one knee. Horus advanced, ready to attack. But Set slammed his fist into the floor, sending a shockwave towards Horus, who was knocked off balance and fell. The ground shook as the God's body hit the flagstones. As Horus struggled to get up and back into the fight, Set raised his arms and howled out a barbaric torrent of words Akori could not understand. Thunder boomed and lightning rippled up and down Set's whole body. He pointed at Horus.

"And now, worthless wretch of a God, you die!" he screamed.

Lightning ripped from his pointing finger

105

through the air towards Horus – and Akori stepped into its path. Blocking it with the Shield of Sekhmet, ignoring the pain from the hissing sparks, he took step after step towards Set.

The dark God roared out another strange word and the arcs of lightning grew stronger, filling the room with the stench of burned metal. Akori's whole arm felt as if it were on fire, but still he advanced, defying Set, defying his fear. Set shrieked, lashing out at Akori with bolt after searing bolt of energy. But still Akori kept coming.

"I am Set!" the evil God bellowed. "I am Lord of Storms! *You will fear me!*"

Akori peered around his shield, preparing for the worst. But just as the evil God reared up to attack, Horus appeared behind Set and restrained him.

"Finish him, Akori!" Horus urged as Set

struggled to free himself. "Banish him back to the Underworld!"

Akori ran forward, *khopesh* at the ready. He swung – but Set was already dissolving into black smoke and fading away. The sword swept through empty air. Horus's fingers closed on nothingness. They were alone.

"Our enemy has fled!" Horus declared, his eyes shining with triumph. "A thousand curses on him for the coward he is. And blessed be the courage of mortal men for ever!"

Akori raised his sword and gave a wordless cry of pure joy. In that moment, he felt he could have lifted the whole earth in the palm of his hand.

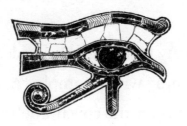

CHAPTER TEN

"I wish there were time to celebrate our victory, but your work is not yet done," said Horus. "One final quest remains."

Akori was puzzled. "But Set was in control...wasn't he? What other evil Gods are left?"

"None," said Horus. "Your last enemy is a mortal like yourself. You must confront Oba. Only when he is defeated can you take your position as the true Pharaoh of Egypt."

The thought left Akori stunned. He had

been so occupied with releasing the good Gods that he hadn't given any thought to what might happen afterwards. Taking the throne, being crowned, then ruling an entire kingdom?

"Pharaoh? But I'd have to make laws, pronounce judgements, deal with politics..." His voice trailed off as uncertainty gripped him. "I wouldn't know where to start."

"I will be there to help you," Horus reminded him.

"I'm not ready to be Pharaoh!" Akori blustered. "Why me? Why now? All I know about is fighting and farming!"

"Akori, listen to me, and know my words for truth," said Horus gravely. "A true Pharaoh is not made only by what knowledge he carries in his head, but also by the worthiness of his heart. You have a brave, loyal and generous heart, my friend. And you have royal blood in your veins."

"Are you *sure* being Pharaoh is my destiny?"

Horus let out a low, booming laugh. "You have freed five of the good Gods of Egypt, a challenge unheard of even in the golden age of the heroes. You have faced down the dark Gods and emerged victorious. Who but the true-born Pharaoh could have done all that?" Horus held out his open hand and light shimmered across the palm. A rainbow-coloured cloak appeared there. Ghostly rays of light streamed out from it, like sunlight shining through a rotating crystal. "Take it," Horus said. "My last gift to you, along with my eternal thanks. This cloak is called the 'Wings of Horus'."

With trembling fingers Akori fastened the cloak around his neck, feeling very royal all of a sudden. "It's beautiful," he said. "So light." Then he laughed. "Why is it called the Wings of Horus? Does it let me fly in the air like a bird?"

"Actually, yes." Horus smiled, and started fading gently into rays of sparkling light. "Farewell until we meet again, and thank you once more."

Akori's eyes widened and a broad smile spread over his face. He strode out of the dungeon, through the corridors, out of the temple and into the open air, his spirits growing stronger all the time. All of his doubts had melted away as soon as he put on the cloak. He felt bold, ready to meet Oba and finish this once and for all.

Manu and Ebe were waiting by the gateway, with anxious looks on their faces. Manu was standing up, clearly recovered from his injury. As soon as Ebe saw Akori, she bounded across the sand to him and hugged him tight.

"You're alive!" Manu yelled excitedly. "What happened? Did you free Horus? Was Set there? What—"

"I'll tell you on the way," Akori interrupted. "We have to get to the Pharaoh's palace."

"But how are we going to get there?" Manu fell into an awed silence as two immense wings unfolded from the cloak on Akori's back, gleaming with bright colours.

"We fly," Akori said with a smile. He held out his hands to his friends. "Both of you, hold on tight."

Ebe and Manu each grabbed one of Akori's arms. The Wings of Horus began to beat, and the three of them sailed up into the air.

Akori turned his head towards the south. That was where Oba was waiting, and no matter how brave Akori was feeling, he knew the Pharaoh would not give up his throne without an almighty fight.

As they soared higher, Egypt spread out beneath them like one of Manu's maps. Akori caught his breath as he looked down upon the golden desert and the glistening Nile. If he became Pharaoh, he would rule all of this. The thought took his breath away.

"There's the palace!" Manu said, pointing down.

Akori twisted the Ring of Isis on his finger so that they became invisible, then they swooped down for a closer look. Even though they were hidden from sight, he still felt nervous, as if arrows and javelins could start flying up at them at any minute.

The palace lay on the banks of the Nile, a huge complex of white buildings surrounded by a high wall with towers. It was well defended, with ranks of soldiers both outside and in. Most of them were clustered around a huge gatehouse at the front.

Akori silently gave a prayer of thanks to Horus for his gift of flight. Oba had obviously expected an attack to come from the ground. Flying down from above, they might have a chance of reaching the palace in one piece.

"Listen," he said. "They're chanting!"

The soldiers were stamping and chanting Oba's name, beating on their shields with their swords.

"They sound like fanatics," Manu said anxiously. "Loyal to the last breath. They'll never surrender."

Akori wondered if they were truly loyal or just terrified of Oba. Down below, he saw the central hub of the palace come into view. In front of it lay a wide sandy courtyard, enclosed by pillared walls. The neglected remains of flower beds lay parched by the sun. Before Oba came, the courtyard must have held ornamental gardens. Now it was nothing but a square for soldiers to march in.

"I'm going to land in that inner courtyard!" he said. "That has to be where the Pharaoh's rooms are. Past those double doors."

Ebe made an agitated whining noise and pointed at a group of soldiers standing in the shadow of the wall.

"I know," Akori said. "They must be Oba's personal guard. We're going to have to sneak past them."

Akori began the descent. He took them in a wide spiral, dropping lower and lower until they were nearly brushing the domed rooftops. Then they glided silently down into the centre of the courtyard.

Standing at the head of the soldiers was a cruel-faced man in priests' robes, holding a staff. Akori guessed who he was immediately – Set's High Priest and Oba's closest ally, Bukhu. He scowled upwards, as if he alone expected the attack to come from the sky and not from the ground.

Still invisible, they landed. Akori had had no practice at this, and his feet made a thudding sound and churned up the sand as he touched down.

Bukhu noticed the disturbance and narrowed his eyes. He shook his staff and spat some words of magic. And, like a cloak being ripped away, their covering of invisibility was suddenly gone.

"Oh, this is bad," Manu said, looking around at all of the soldiers glaring at them. "Very bad."

Bukhu grinned, showing yellow teeth. "I see you, farm boy! You shouldn't be playing with magic. You might get hurt."

Akori stood in a battle stance. "I am Akori, the true Pharaoh," he announced. "I have freed Horus and all the good Gods, and now I'm here to defeat Oba." He raised his voice. "The false Pharaoh who rules through fear and lies!"

The soldiers muttered uneasily.

"You all know it's true!" Akori shouted at them. "But nobody has the courage to say so, do they?"

The soldiers looked at one another, as if they wished someone would speak. Nobody did. Akori could feel their loyalty to Oba hanging by a thread. The news that Horus was free had shaken them.

"Oba wants you dead or alive," Bukhu snarled to Akori. "It doesn't matter which."

"Fight by my side, or lay down your weapons and get out of my way!" Akori said to the soldiers, ignoring Bukhu. "I can offer

119

you a better future. Be sensible and take it while you can."

A handful of the soldiers moved away from the others and approached Akori.

"You have freed all of the good Gods?" one of them asked him.

Akori nodded. "Including Horus, who was guarded by Set himself. It was Horus who gave me this cloak, so that I might fly here today and save all of Egypt from Oba."

A murmur of admiration rippled through the soldiers. One of them even saluted him. Akori felt hope lift his heart. Then another group broke away to join him, and then another.

Bukhu scowled. "Charge them!" he yelled frantically to the remaining soldiers. "Cut them down!"

The soldiers charged. Akori cursed under his breath. Wild fighting broke out all around him. Some of the soldiers fought each other, but most of them attacked Akori. The Shield of Sekhmet rang with the impact of blow after deadly blow. He parried, dodged, parried again...but there were so many! He lost sight of Manu and Ebe in the crowd.

A group of soldiers tried to surround him, with Bukhu urging them on. "A bag of gold for whoever brings me the boy's head!" he yelled.

Akori was backed into a corner, with half a dozen soldiers thrusting spears at him. He fought desperately, trying to think of some way out. But every exit was closed off and he faced a seemingly endless army of warriors.

A spear point caught him on the cheek, painfully drawing blood. He sliced the end off the spear, leaving the soldier with a useless pole. Filled with rage, he was about to cut the man down when Bukhu's triumphant voice rang out:

"Surrender now, boy, or watch your friend die!"

Bukhu had Manu's arm twisted up behind his back. He was holding a dagger at his throat. Manu's eyes were wide with fear, begging Akori to do something.

"No! Don't hurt him!" Akori yelled. If Manu's throat was cut, even the Scarab of Anubis wouldn't be able to save him! There was no way to reach Manu in time, even if he flew.

Bukhu shrugged. "So be it." He held the struggling Manu pinned, ready to kill him with one swift stroke.

A roar resounded across the courtyard.

Everyone turned in shock.

Akori was dumbfounded. It was the same roar they had heard in the desert, from the

creature that had saved them from Anat and
Astarte! How could it be here, too?

The soldiers started backing off from
something, fighting to get away. A widening
gap was appearing in the battle. In its centre
stood—

"*Ebe?*" Akori gasped. He couldn't believe
his eyes. Ebe's whole body was changing.
Her arms and legs grew long, the fingernails
and toenails extending into claws. Tawny fur
began covering her face. Terrified soldiers
were screaming and running away at the
sight.

Ebe fell to all fours, roaring, no longer a
mute slave girl, but a gigantic wildcat – the
very same beast that had saved Manu's life
in the desert, chasing away the evil wives
of Set.

Akori thought back to their very first
quest, when he had been at the mercy of the

Snake Goddess Wadjet. A catlike creature had helped them then, too, coming out of nowhere to protect them.

It had been Ebe all along!

CHAPTER ELEVEN

Rank upon rank of soldiers turned and fled from Ebe the giant wildcat. They crashed through the outer gates and ran, yelling. Their panic was catching; more and more of Oba's royal guard saw the terror and fled themselves, afraid of what might be coming after them.

"Stand your ground, men!" Bukhu bellowed. "It's an illusion! A stupid trick!"

But no one listened to him. In a matter of moments, not a single soldier was left. The dusty courtyard was littered with abandoned shields and spears. Only Bukhu himself had dared to stay, his knife still at Manu's throat. Ebe crouched down, snarling menacingly.

Bukhu tightened his grip on Manu and began to edge back towards the palace. "Move and he dies!" he shrieked. "I mean it!"

Akori slipped the Talisman of Ra into his hand. "Mighty Ra, send me light!" he prayed.

A dazzling beam flashed into Bukhu's eyes. He covered his face to save his sight – and Manu slipped free.

Quick as a flash, Ebe sprang. She landed on Bukhu hard, knocking him sprawling in the dust. His staff went flying. Ebe's clawed paw shot out and held his thrashing body down like a cat pinning a desert rat.

Bukhu howled in pain and fear. "Mercy! I beg you...mercy!"

Manu rubbed his neck. Then he picked up Bukhu's staff and broke it across his knee.

There was a hiss and a faint wailing sound, like many tormented voices crying out at once. A host of freed spirits went spiralling up from the broken staff, fading in the bright sunshine.

Ebe raised one great paw, ready to strike and end Bukhu's life quickly and cleanly. Bukhu was sobbing with fear now.

"No, Ebe," said Manu. "It's all right, his power is broken."

"But he tried to kill you!" Akori yelled.

Ebe looked at Manu questioningly with her great golden eyes.

"He's nothing now," Manu said. "He's not worth killing."

"Oh, thank you, merciful priest of Horus," Bukhu blubbered. "Thank you."

Ebe let him go and he scrambled to his feet.

As Bukhu limped away, Akori saw something glint in the sunlight. Bukhu still had his knife. And he was turning around!

"Manu, look out!" Akori yelled.

Manu dodged out of the way just in time and the knife went flying past him – straight for Akori! Akori lifted his shield. There was a clink as the knife hit the metal and the shield glowed with light suddenly – then came a piercing cry. Akori looked over the shield and saw Bukhu lying on the floor. The knife had rebounded and was embedded in his chest. Bukhu would never speak again.

Manu was staring wide-eyed at Bukhu's body. Akori touched his shoulder and Manu swallowed, then met his friend's eyes, and nodded. Akori's quest was not over yet.

His heart pounding, Akori left Manu and Ebe guarding the entrance, and quietly slipped into the palace. He was finally about to come face-to-face with Oba. He knew the Pharaoh would be expecting him, but he didn't know what kind of evil tricks he had in store. He had to be prepared. Gripping his shield and sword tightly, he made his way along the corridors of the palace. The walls were alive with colour, with floral and lotus designs blazing from the white plaster. Ornamental chairs with soft cushions were set against the walls for visiting ambassadors to sit on. Bowls on pedestals overflowed with fruit. Where in this luxurious warren was Oba hiding?

Slaves peeped out from doorways as Akori passed, whispering to each other. Were they afraid *for* him or *of* him? He couldn't tell. There were no more guards, only empty room after empty room. Akori stayed alert, watching for ambushes and traps. There had been too many surprises already and he was not going to be tricked again. Eventually, deep within the palace, he came to a set of double doors covered with carvings. A young slave girl waited outside, clutching her arms, her eyes full of fear. She saw Akori, ran to him and fell on her knees.

"The one you seek is inside," she said, her voice low and trembling. "He is alone, but not alone."

"What do you mean?" Akori asked.

The girl shook her braided head as if she had said too much. She beckoned him close and whispered in his ear, "May the good Gods go with you."

Then she was gone, running on silent feet, vanishing up the hallway like a ghost. Gripping his *khopesh* and shield tightly, Akori kicked the doors open.

It was dark in the private chamber of Oba the Pharaoh, as it always was. Flames flickered in the fire basket, casting dancing shadows. Akori waited on the threshold, wary. He took in the details of the room. Every surface glistened with rich colour. Gold ornaments, black polished wood, blue crystal...it was a treasure house as well as a bedchamber. The air was thick with mixed scents; jasmine and rose, and under it all the bitter dark odour of myrrh. On a nearby bench, hundreds of bottles of scented oils shone in the firelight. Then something moved in the darkness at the back of the room, like a crocodile at the bottom of a murky pool. Akori tensed. He could just make out the figure of a young boy on a couch. Pale eyes rimmed with black looked back at him, as if the darkness were wearing a human mask.

"I've been expecting you," sneered the high-born voice, then added, "farm boy."

A crescent of silver appeared in the darkness as Oba drew his sword. Graceful as a panther, he advanced.

"It took you long enough to find my chamber," Oba said. "What happened?"

Akori said nothing. He breathed hard and fast. A bead of sweat began to trickle down his face. The heat from the fire was like a furnace. Oba's body shone in the firelight as he moved closer. His chest was bare, gleaming with oil. All he wore was a black woven *shendyt*. He was obviously used to the heat.

Akori quickly judged the distance between them. He wasn't quite close enough to reach him with his sword. He stood his ground, waiting for Oba to get nearer.

"Don't you know how to talk, farm boy?"

Oba's sing-song voice rang in Akori's ears.

His belly was full of anger and it was boiling over.

"Shut up and fight!" Akori roared.

"A miracle. The idiot can speak."

Feeling a flash of rage, Akori lashed out too soon. Oba easily knocked the clumsy blow aside. He swung at Akori, but his blade clanged off the Shield of Sekhmet.

"Brave little Akori, hiding behind your magical toys," Oba sneered. "But you dare not face me man to man."

Then Oba attacked, viciously and fast. He came at Akori from the sides, from above – his blade seemed to be everywhere!

Akori could only retreat, holding up the shield to ward off the hacking, slashing blade. The heat was intense. Sweat was running into his eyes. Oba dodged back and forth like a dancer. His soft, mocking laughter never stopped. Akori tried to attack, but only managed another clumsy swipe. Oba leaped back from it nimbly.

"You fight like a peasant reaping wheat!" he sneered. "You never learned how to use a weapon, did you?"

Akori backed up further, clenching his jaw hard. Oba's constant taunts were driving him wild with rage. He felt the bench of scented oils press against the back of his legs. If he let Oba drive him any further back, he'd trip over it.

"A farm boy from farmer stock!" Oba spat, slicing as he spoke. "But the farm isn't doing so well these days, is it? You ran away, and your poor old Uncle Shenti got killed!"

"Shut up!"

Oba pursed his lips. "Such a tragedy for a poor hard-working family..."

Akori snapped. *"Your men murdered him!"* he screamed at the top of his voice.

He dropped the Shield of Sekhmet and grasped his sword two-handed, like a scythe. If Oba wanted to see how a farm boy could fight, Akori would show him. Roaring madly, he slashed and struck.

Oba barely managed to get out of the way in time. Cushions split. Feathers flew. Akori might have been backed up against the wall, but he was coming out fighting like a madman!

It was sword against sword now. Oba was skilled, but Akori was strong. Even when Oba blocked Akori's blows, the force of them made him stagger. Time and again the golden sword hummed past Oba's head, close, so very close.

"Not laughing any more, eh?" Akori yelled, his mind a pure red fury. His sword was a golden blur.

Oba dodged, just avoiding a severed arm.

Then, with lethal speed, Oba lunged. His sword caught Akori's at the guard, and locked. Oba gave a vicious twist and the *khopesh* was torn out of Akori's grip. It fell to the floor.

Akori tried to grab it back, but Oba's sword was suddenly levelled at his face. Oba bent and picked up the *khopesh*, exchanging it for his own sword, which he threw to the back of the room.

"Our little game is over," he said with a smirk. "Clod. Dung-head. I knew you would not be able to resist my trap."

"Trap?" said Akori numbly.

"I knew you would come looking for me here, alone! That's how you thought it would work, isn't it? Just you and me? A heroic duel to the death?" Oba backed away towards the fire. "Stand still, you fool, and prepare yourself. We're about to have company."

"Company?" Akori tried to guess what he meant. "Your High Priest, Bukhu, is dead. Didn't they tell you? He won't be coming to help!"

Oba laughed mockingly. "Not him! That useless idiot got what he deserved. I'm talking about Set himself! The Lord of Storms will be finishing you off personally, once I have called him from his sacred fire!"

Akori glanced at the flames and forced himself to be calm. He kept his eyes on Oba, but he began to move his hand stealthily behind his back towards the bench full of oils.

"What will you do now, with none of your precious Gods to help you?" Oba snarled.

"Set has fallen already," Akori said. "Horus defeated him. With my help."

Oba's face twisted in hate. "Liar! A weakling like you couldn't—"

Akori seized his chance. He grabbed a huge bottle of scented oil from the bench and flung it at Oba's feet.

Oba leaped to avoid it – and came down on the spreading puddle of oil. His bare feet skidded and slipped.

Akori dived across the room and grabbed Oba's wrist. He pulled Oba down, sending him sprawling. Then he bashed Oba's hand against the edge of the fire basket until he let the *khopesh* go. Akori snatched it up. Oba struggled to stand up, still slipping about in the oil. "Come forth from the fire, Lord of Darkness, Mighty Set!" he cried desperately. *"Help meeeee!"*

Summoning his last drop of strength Akori thrust out with his *khopesh*.

Oba's eyes widened. Blood began to mingle with the oil at his feet. All at once, Oba fell, limp as a rag doll.

But Akori barely had time to draw breath before the embers in the fire basket began to stir! From the midst of the fire Set arose, breaking up through the charcoal like a figure of volcanic rock rising from a burning sea, terrible in his anger.

Set had been horrific before, but now he was out for revenge, and there was no terror on earth like him. Hairs bristled like needles on his massive body. His lips peeled back from his huge yellow teeth in a beast-like snarl, and threads of drool trailed to the floor, sizzling in the heat. Hellfire surrounded his dark form, burning like a halo.

Akori took a step back in horror, grabbing for the Shield of Sekhmet that lay on the floor.

"Boy. Idiot boy. Did you really think you could defeat me?" Set bellowed.

The room filled with sulphurous smoke,

making Akori cough and his eyes water. Set stepped out of the fire, the floor smouldering under his tread. He loomed before Akori like a vengeful genie, with Oba's limp form at his feet.

Akori brandished his *khopesh*. It was all he could think to do.

"Get ready to meet your Gods!" Set roared. He raised a huge fist.

Akori knew he could not possibly survive. Even the Shield of Sekhmet could not protect him from such a blow.

Set's fist was coming down on him.

"Akori, your Gods are already with you," said a voice from behind.

Light filled the chamber – dazzling light, bright as the noonday sun.

Set reeled back, blinded and roaring in confusion. Akori turned around, awed. He knew that voice.

There, surrounded by glory, was Ra, God of the Sun. Beside him stood jackal-headed Anubis, and the beautiful Goddess Isis, smiling her gentle smile. Lion-headed Sekhmet was roaring out a greeting. Beside her stood Horus, restored to his full power, radiating light that should have been blinding. And yet Akori could see clearly.

All five of the good Gods who Akori had freed were here!

"You did not fail us when we needed you most, Akori," Horus said. "Nor shall we fail you in your hour of need."

"Fools! I shall destroy you all!" Set raged. "I am unvanquishable! *I am Set!*"

"You cannot win against us, dark brother," said Isis softly. "We stand united. Our powers are as one."

"Begone!" roared Sekhmet. "You have lost the battle!"

"All your darkness cannot protect you from the powers of light," said Ra, his fists burning with golden energy.

"Wherever you run," growled jackal-headed Anubis, "and wherever you hide, I shall find you. Go! Crawl back to the Underworld, and do not trouble humanity again!"

Set grabbed Oba's body from the floor. To Akori's surprise, Oba moaned faintly. He was still alive!

"Enjoy your victory!" Set hissed. "It will be short-lived, I promise you that! We will return!"

Carrying Oba with him, Set jumped into the flames. The fire flared up hot and red, spewing foul-smelling black smoke. Then they were gone, to the Underworld, and the room was silent once more.

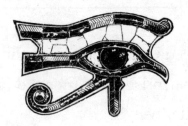

CHAPTER TWELVE

"Thank you!" Akori burst out. "I thought I was dead for certain!"

"After all you have done for us," said Ra, "we could hardly stand back and do nothing."

The other Gods nodded agreement. Together they walked back to the courtyard. Behind them, amazed servants followed, pointing at the Gods. Some raised their voices in songs of worship, and many fell to their knees and wept with joy.

Akori threw open the doors to the courtyard, letting the bright sun flood in. Manu came running up, but stopped in his tracks when he saw the Gods standing there.

"We won, Manu!" Akori said. "Oba is gone. Set is defeated. It's over!"

Manu tried to speak, but couldn't. He looked from one God to another, his eyes filled with amazement. Akori grinned and clapped him on the shoulder. "I couldn't have done it without you, Manu. I owe you my life."

In the middle of the courtyard, Ebe the huge wildcat was rolling on her back, enjoying the sunshine. When she noticed Akori, she rolled over. Very slowly, she stood up, and began walking on her hind legs. Her body started to shrink, becoming more human, until she was a woman with a cat's head. Akori and Manu looked at each other, then walked over to her. She raised a hand in greeting.

"Hello, old friends."

"Are you still Ebe?" Akori asked, doubtfully.

"Not any more," she purred. "That dream is over."

"Then who are you?" Akori said.

"Men know me as the Goddess Bast," she explained. "Horus asked me to take on a human form, in order to help you on your quest. So I became Ebe, and waited in the Temple of Horus until the day you came."

Manu looked puzzled. "But how could you have known Akori was going to come to the Temple?"

"It was his destiny," said Bast simply. "Horus told me so."

"You saved our lives," Manu said.

"And you saved mine!" replied Bast.

"While I was human, the dangers I faced were real."

"I'll miss Ebe," sighed Akori. "She was a good friend."

"And she always will be," Bast said with a smile. "Never doubt it. Now, listen to Horus. He has something to tell you."

All eyes turned to Horus, who raised his arms to the sky.

"Hail, Akori!" he shouted, his voice echoing through the palace grounds. "Hail the new Pharaoh! Let Egypt know peace and prosperity once more. Evil has been defeated and banished to the Underworld!"

A mighty cheer went up. Soldiers on the walls threw down their spears and roared Akori's name. All the Gods bowed their heads in respect.

Akori felt very strange. Was all this really for him?

151

"It is time to live out your destiny," Horus told him. "Remember what was said in the Prophecy of the Sphinx? A hero of the wheatfields will rule all Egypt. That hero is you, Akori."

EPILOGUE

A few days had passed. From all over Egypt, people had been pouring into the city of Waset. All the taverns and inns were full, and some people were camping out on the rooftops and in the streets, but nobody complained. Their new Pharaoh was to be crowned today.

A lucky few thousand had been able to get into the palace courtyard, to witness the procession setting off to the Karnak Temple. Many noble families were surprised to find the very best seats of all had been given to ordinary people – fishermen, cobblers, even farmers – by order of the new Pharaoh. So the nobles had to be content with standing around while the commoners sat in comfort, drinking to the Pharaoh's health with barley beer every ten minutes. None of the noblemen complained about it though. Evil had finally been banished, and it was time to celebrate.

Out of sight of the crowds, in a room just off the courtyard, Akori was pacing up and down, dressed in a plain white robe. The aged High Priest entered, and Akori embraced him fondly.

"I'm so glad you could come!" he said. "It was such a long way!"

The High Priest waved his concern aside. "With all respect, Akori, hush. I would not have missed this day for anything."

"I do have something to ask of you," Akori said. "Would you stay here, with me, at the palace? I need a High Priest here, and I can't think of anyone better than you."

"I am honoured!" the High Priest said.

"But I fear I am too old for such a position. My life is reaching its end, and your reign is about to begin." He thought for a moment. "But I do believe I know just the right person for the job. Manu, are you here?"

Manu stepped out of the shadows. "I am."

"You have shown great bravery," the High Priest said. "Much greater, I admit, than I ever expected. I hereby declare your apprenticeship at an end. You are now a fully ordained Priest of Horus. Serve well."

Akori and Manu looked at one another with delight.

"And I strongly recommend," the High Priest continued, his blind eyes twinkling, "that Manu be appointed as High Priest to the Pharaoh himself."

"I'm only too happy to accept your recommendation!" Akori said with a smile.

Manu beamed with delight. "Thank you.

Thank you. It would be an honour." Then he frowned. "Of course if I am to be your High Priest, I will need some more scrolls."

Akori laughed loudly. "Manu, as my priest you shall have all the scrolls your heart desires!"

Manu chuckled, then he peeked round a pillar into the courtyard. "It's a beautiful day, you know."

Akori nodded. "It is."

"There's quite a crowd out there."

"Well," said Akori with a nervous sigh, "I suppose we'd better go and meet them. Coming?"

A huge cheer went up from the crowd as Akori and Manu emerged into the sunlight. The people waved and threw garlands of flowers down at them. Songs were sung, Akori's name was chanted, and the good Gods were praised. All across the city, the sound of *celebration rose up into the clear blue sky.*

Clear and blue it was, all across the dome of heaven...all except for one small black cloud near the horizon, which all the bright sunshine could not quite banish.

Also available:

ATTACK OF THE SCORPION RIDERS

For his first quest, Akori must risk his life, fighting giant scorpions and a deadly Snake Goddess. But will his terrifying battle end in victory?

ISBN 9781409521051

CURSE OF THE DEMON DOG

The dead are stalking the living and Akori must send them back to their graves. But dog-headed Am-Heh the Hunter has sworn to destroy Akori...

ISBN 9781409521068

BATTLE OF THE CROCODILE KING

Akori must brave the crocodile-infested waters of the Nile to battle the terrifying Crocodile King, and his gruesome wife, the bloodthirsty Frog Goddess.

ISBN 9781409521075

LAIR OF THE WINGED MONSTER

Vicious vultures and deadly beasts lie in wait for Akori as he searches the desert for the Hidden Fortress of Fire – and the Goddess imprisoned there.

ISBN 9781409521082

COLLECT THE CARDS AND PLAY THE GAMES!

HIGHER OR LOWER

Players: 2
Number of cards: 8+
Instructions:

- Shuffle the pack and place it face down on the table. Roll a dice to see who starts.
- *Player One*: turn the first card over, placing it next to the deck, and choose a category.
- *Player Two*: guess if the score on the next card for the chosen category will be higher or lower, then turn over the next card in the pack, and place it next to the first. If you guessed correctly, you win the combined score of both stats. If you guessed wrongly, you score 0. Then return the two cards in play to the bottom of the pack.
- Now swap over, so that Player Two turns over the next card and chooses a category, and Player One guesses higher or lower. Repeat for 4 rounds, then add up your total scores.
- *WIN:* The player with the most points wins!

DOWNLOAD SCORESHEETS AND FIND MORE GAMES AT WWW.QUESTOFTHEGODS.CO.UK